DISNEY'S
Aladdin

Who's That Ghost?

DISNEY PRESS

New York

It was a dark, rainy day in Agrabah. "I wish we could take a walk outside," Jasmine said with a sigh.

"Don't let the bad weather get you down," Aladdin replied. "We can walk through the palace. Abu, why don't you come, too?"

The Genie overheard the plan. "I think it's time for a little rainy-day fun!" he told himself with a laugh.

Aladdin led the way. "This hallway will take us to the kitchen," he said. "So, when we're done with our walk, we can have a snack."

But then Aladdin took a wrong turn. The air began to feel cold and damp, and the hallway grew dark.

Aladdin spotted a door up ahead. "That must be the door to the kitchen," he said, relieved.

THIS
WAY
TO
THE
KITCHEN

He slowly opened the door. Suddenly, hundreds of squealing bats flew out and circled around.

"Let's get out of here!" yelled Jasmine.

The three friends ran until they came to another door. "In here!" shouted Aladdin. They ran inside.

Aladdin was sure this was the way to the kitchen. But a few more steps led them into the dark, cold, spooky palace dungeon.

As they decided what to do next, the sound of laughter surrounded them. A voice boomed, "Even if you scream and shout, I don't think I'll let you out!"

"Who are you?" asked Aladdin.

"Here I am—your lovely host. I'm the creepy dungeon ghost!" the voice shouted. They couldn't believe their eyes—it was a ghost!

All of a sudden, the ghost disappeared.

"Don't worry," Aladdin told Jasmine and Abu. "I'll get us out of here safely."

They cautiously made their way through the dungeon's twists and turns. They had reached a dead end when the floor suddenly gave way.

"*Aaaaahhhhhh!*" screamed Aladdin, Jasmine, and Abu as they went flying down a chute. They finally landed with a thump.

The ghost appeared again. "Nice trip?" it said.

Aladdin and Jasmine looked at each other. This ghost was starting to remind them of someone they knew.

"Hey, do we know you?" asked Aladdin.

"I'll say!" the ghost said with a chuckle.

Jasmine turned to Aladdin and raised her eyebrows. Aladdin looked closely at the ghost. There was something *very* familiar about it.

"And do you know who I am?" asked Jasmine.

"Yeah, you're Princess Jasmine—Al's girl!" answered the ghost.

"Aha!" shouted Aladdin.

"You're not a ghost. You're the Genie!" Jasmine cried.

"Oops, caught me!" said the Genie, turning back into himself. "I lose!"

"That wasn't very funny, Genie," said Aladdin.

"Yeah, you really scared us," said Jasmine.

"I'm sorry," said the Genie. "But you did say you were bored. It was just a little rainy-day fun."

Jasmine and Aladdin couldn't help but laugh.

"Now, can you get us out of here?" asked Aladdin.

"Yes, sir," said the Genie as he quickly turned into a giant flashlight and led them to the kitchen.

Soon they were happily eating ice-cream sundaes.

"I guess I did a pretty good job of scaring up some ice cream," said the Genie.

Everyone laughed. A boring rainy day with the Genie around? Never!